Nosy Rosy

Nosy Rosy

Peter Curry

Collins

An imprint of HarperCollins*Publishers*

Nosy Rosy went down the lane to see who was there...

Who's that
having lunch?

Gosh! Aren't you greedy!

Don't be so nosy, Rosy!

Who's that in the garden?

That was a big kiss!

Don't be so nosy, Rosy!

Who's that putting out the washing?

What big pants!

Who's that singing?

La La La Di Da . . .

What a lot
of bubbles!

Don't be so nosy, Rosy!

Who's that in
Mr Tiger's shop?

TOYS

That's not Mr Tiger!

we're glad you're so nosy!

First published in paperback in Great Britain by Collins Picture Books in 2001
1 3 5 7 9 10 8 6 4 2
ISBN: 0 00 664724 3
Text and illustrations copyright © Peter Curry 2000
The author/illustrator asserts the moral right to be identified as the author/illustrator of the work.
A CIP catalogue record for this title is available from the British Library.

The HarperCollins website address is: www.fireandwater.com

Manufactured in China

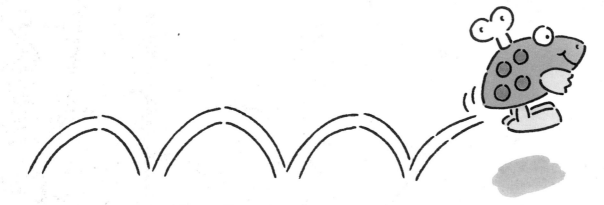

Little Pig Figwort
HENRIETTA BRANFORD
ILLUSTRATED BY
CLAUDIO MUÑOZ

Whose House?
A lift-the-flap book
Colin and Jacqui Hawkins

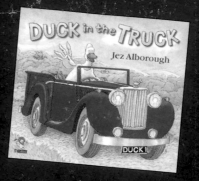
DUCK in the TRUCK
Jez Alborough
DUCK 1

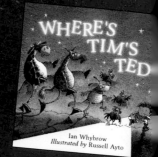
WHERE'S TIM'S TED
Ian Whybrow
Illustrated by Russell Ayto

Every child deserves the best...

Mucky Pup
KEN BROWN

Collins

Picture books

I Love You, Blue Kangaroo!
EMMA CHICHESTER CLARK
shortlisted for the prestigious Kate Greenaway Medal.

The Tiger Who Came to Tea
30th Anniversary Edition
JUDITH KERR

THE SECOND PRINCESS
2
Hiawyn Oram and Tony Ross

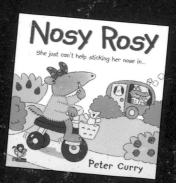
Nosy Rosy
She just can't help sticking her nose in...
Peter Curry

snore!
Michael Rosen & Jonathan Langley